CAN YOU TEACH A FISH TO CLIMB A TREE?

Jane Godwin AND Terry Denton

Bright Light

Hardie Grant Children's Publishing

While the quote that inspired this book is often attributed to Albert Einstein, it is now widely accepted that he never said it. The origin of the quote is unclear, but the words and the wisdom have struck a chord with many, including us!

– Jane Godwin & Terry Denton

For Lizzie, who can do many wonderful things – JG
For Georgia, Lucy and Charlie – TD

Hardie Grant acknowledges the Traditional Owners of the Country on which we work, the Wurundjeri People of the Kulin Nation and the Gadigal People of the Eora Nation, and recognizes their continuing connection to the land, waters and culture. We pay our respects to their Elders past and present.

Bright Light
an imprint of Hardie Grant Children's Publishing
Wurundjeri Country
Ground Floor, Building 1, 658 Church Street
Richmond, Victoria 3121, Australia
Melbourne | Sydney | London | San Francisco
www.hardiegrantchildrens.com

ISBN: 9781761213380

First published in Australia in 2023
This edition published in 2024

Text copyright © 2023 Jane Godwin
Illustration copyright © 2023 Terry Denton
Design copyright © 2023 Hardie Grant Children's Publishing

Design Kristy Lund-White
Editorial Johanna Gogos and Luna Soo
Production Sally Davis

With thanks to Hannah Givens, sensitivity consultant.

Printed in China by Leo Paper Group

5 4 3 2 1

FSC
www.fsc.org
MIX
Paper | Supporting responsible forestry
FSC® C020056

The paper this book is printed on is from FSC®-certified forests and other sources. FSC® promotes environmentally responsible, socially beneficial and economically viable management of the world's forests.

Can you teach a fish to climb a tree?

If a bird practiced all day and all night,
could she write her name?

Could a dog play the violin?

Or a hippo walk a tightrope?

Do you think a lizard could ever learn to sail a boat?

Could you teach a seal to fly?

Or penguins to sing opera?

Could a baby bake a cake?

Or a horse drive a car?

No? Then what's wrong with them all?

What *can* they do?

Well…

Fish can make shapes when they swim,
each in their own special place.

Hippos can run and leap underwater.

Penguins can keep each other warm in the coldest place on Earth.

Horses can sleep standing up.

Could you do that?

Lizards are excellent at hiding. Can you see this one?

A bird can fly from one end of the world...

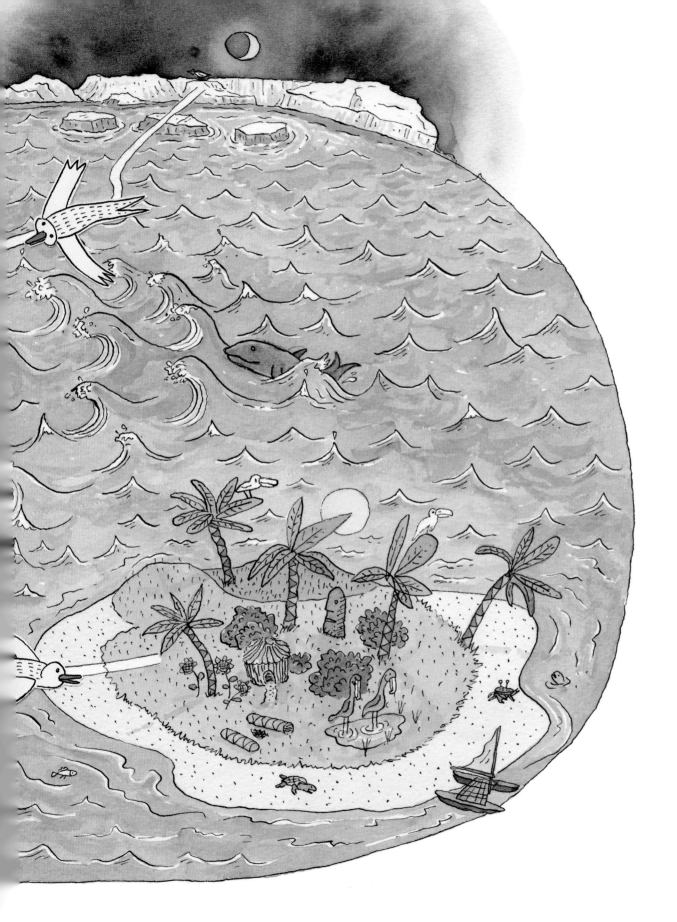

...to the other, without ever getting lost.

Seals can hold their
breath for two whole hours!

A baby can learn to speak just by copying other people.

A dog can be a good and loyal friend.

And you?

You can do wonderful things, too.

It's true.

What do YOU like to do?